Contents

Farm Stories

Written by Gill Davies

Illustrated by Angelika Scudamore

First published 2016 by Brown Watson

The Old Mill, 76 Fleckney Road

Kibworth Beauchamp

Leicestershire LE8 0HG

ISBN: 978-0-7097-2379-0

Reprinted 2017

Printed in Malaysia

Brown Watson

ENGLAND

Tommy Tractor

Tiny Tommy Tractor does everything he can to help his big friend Ed. Whenever Ed is bored or tired, Tommy cheers him up. He makes Ed laugh when he is sad … and when Ed has a puncture, it is Tommy who scurries off to fetch him a spare tyre.

One day Tommy whispers, "Would you like to know a secret, Ed?
The hens have vanished!"
"Oh no!" sighs Ed. "But I know where they are," giggles Tommy,
"They are tucked up inside your truck, all cosy under the hay."
"Really!" cries Ed, "I had no idea. We must take
them back straight away."

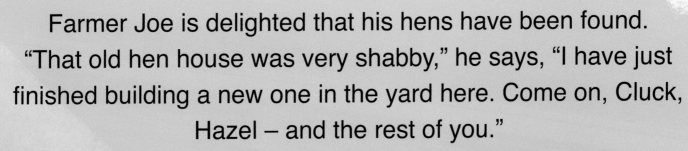

Farmer Joe is delighted that his hens have been found.
"That old hen house was very shabby," he says, "I have just
finished building a new one in the yard here. Come on, Cluck,
Hazel – and the rest of you."
Once the hens are happily settled in, Joe says,
"Thanks, Ed and Tommy. Now have a day off. You deserve it."
So the two smiling tractors roll up into the hills to
enjoy the sunshine together.

Clara's Concert

Clara loves music. She shakes her head until the little bell under her chin jingles and jangles. Then she moos gently and sways in the breeze, tapping her hooves on the grass. Most of all she loves to trot around the farm house and peep in through the window to watch the talent shows on television.

"Oh, I do so want to be a singing star!" she sighs.

So you can imagine how excited she is when Farmer Jo leaves his radio behind in the barn one day. The happy little cow dances all day until darkness falls. She moos along to the music as all the little mice clap.
Then Clara announces, her eyes dancing with delight,
"I am going to hold a concert."

The next day all the animals gather to watch. Clara moos so beautifully that everyone cheers. Next Clara invites the other animals to join in so they take it in turns to grunt or neigh or miaow, to baa and cock-a-doodle doo – and dance in time to the radio. "That was the very best day of my life!" sighs Clara happily, as she trots home.

Timid Tiny

Timid Tiny Turkey is frightened of noises. She scoots for cover whenever the tractor starts or if the cows moo too loudly. Farmer Fred found Tiny one day at market.

She had run away and was hiding under his fruit stall, trying to escape from all the crowds and shouting. No-one came to claim her so he took Timid Tiny home.

All the farm animals were soon her friends and she was very happy... Until one day Farmer Fred said, "Tiny, I want to take you with me to the market. Would you like that?"

"No, I would not like that," thought Tiny. "I just want to stay here where I feel nice and safe." But the farmer took no notice of her sad little face and, in no time at all, Tiny found herself riding off in the tractor.

The next day all the animals were amazed to see that
Tiny was wearing a show rosette – an award for bravery.
"Tiny was a hero," explained Farmer Fred. "She was looking
after the stall while I had lunch. Some naughty boys tried to steal
the fruit but Tiny pecked them and flapped at their ankles until
they ran away!" Well done, Tiny!

Thirsty Work

It is the hottest summer day. The farm animals slip into the shadows under the trees to stay cool. The farm children have lots of milk and orange juice. Mrs Jolly drinks tea. Farmer Jolly swills back a large glass of sweet cider. The cats and the sheepdog lap up their water. Timmy Tractor is fine. He is in the cool barn and has plenty of petrol and water in his system to keep him running well.

Farmer Jolly opens the barn door. Golden sunlight streams in. "Hello Timmy," he says, "We are going somewhere special today." Outside the lanes are full of blossom. Bees sip nectar, ready to make honey. Flowers dazzle and gleam but long for the morning dew. Farmer Jolly drives under an arch into an orchard.

Everyone is busy collecting apples and pears. "These fruits will be
wonderful to eat," says Farmer Jolly, "And we shall also be able
to make juice – and cider!" he adds with a grin. It is such a busy
day but, at last, as the sun sets and paints the sky pink,
all the fruit has been collected.
Timmy and his friends toot goodbye to each other and then
trundle home through the sleepy lanes.

Hens Don't Fly Much

There was once a tiny, fluffy, little yellow chick called Chloe who wanted to fly. Each morning Chloe watched the birds that zoomed down to the fence to chirrup and call. How she longed to join them as they took to the air again. "We hens don't fly much," her mother explained. "We don't need to. Everything we could possibly want is right here."

"Don't you wish you could fly?" Chloe asked Sammy Dog.
"No," barked Sammy. "I like to keep my four paws firmly on the
ground but I can run really fast. Hold on tight and I'll show you."
Then Sammy jumped up and over the wall and ran all the way to
the scarecrow and back with Chloe, squealing with joy,
hanging on tightly to his head.

"Don't you wish you could fly?" Chloe asked Harriet Horse. "No," neighed Harriet. "But I can race really fast. Hold on tight and I'll show you." Then Harriet charged all the way to the forest with Chloe clinging tightly to her head. Chloe giggled and squealed: "This is as good as flying. Please can we gallop every day?"
"Of course," Harriet agreed, "It is great fun for me too!"

The Storm

Dolly the Donkey and Whiskers the Cat were the best of friends and always played happily together. Daisy Duck, however, was often bossy and rude. One hot day, when Dolly was panting and Whiskers was too thirsty to think, Daisy Duck quacked crossly, "Go and fetch my sunhat, will you! Quickly!"
Then she settled to sleep in the shade of a tree as the two friends set off.

It was a long way back. On they went – through the grass, along the path, across the pretty little bridge, and around to the pond where Daisy's sunhat was hanging in the reeds. However, just as they were about to trot back again, an almighty storm began. Dolly and Whiskers ran to shelter in the barn.

28

Poor Daisy Duck, however, was all alone and frightened. She crouched under the tree as the lightning flashed and thunder roared. She was terrified. "That loud storm is telling me off for being so selfish and mean," she thought. From that day onwards Daisy tried really hard to be kind and not to be so bossy. So now the three good friends all play happily together down by the stream.

Is Anyone Scared of Sam?

"You don't scare us at all!" cried the noisy crows and the smaller birds. "Will you please pretend to be frightened," begged Sam, "Or the farmer will be cross and put me back in the dark shed. I like it out here in the sunshine!"
So the birds pretended to be scared and flew away.

"Well done, Sam!" said Farmer Giles, as he drove by on his tractor.
"All the crows have flown away. Good work!"
Sam grinned but after a while he began to feel lonely. There was no
one to talk to now that all the birds had vanished. Soon, however,
the bees and butterflies came zooming along to say hello.
"Please tell your other friends to call by," Sam said.

"The trouble with being a scarecrow is that I can't go anywhere," muttered Sam in his empty field. "I am stuck on a pole and have to wait for everyone to remember me."
Soon, however, the bees and butterflies came back – and with them came the harvest mice and the rabbits. That night, the barn owl flew down for a chat. Now the animals all take it in turns to visit Sam so he is never ever lonely.

Lolly Lamb's Mistake

It is summertime. The sky is bluer than bluebells. The corn is high.
Bright red poppies dot the fields. Lolly Lamb is bored. There is
nothing to do and everyone else is too hot to play. So Lolly decides
to chase butterflies. They flutter in between the golden corn.
She jumps as high as her little legs allow but she cannot
catch her fast little friends.

Lolly spots something brown and whiskery dangling between the corn... She chases it. She jumps up really high to catch it in her mouth and gives the whiskery thing a sharp little tug.
"Ow! Stop it!" cries Herbert Horse. It is his tail Lolly is hanging onto. "Oooops! Sorry!" says Lolly. "I thought it was a flower."
"Hah!" Herbert laughs loudly "My tail – a flower. Ha-ha-ha!"

Lolly's mummy hears the noise and trots over to see what is happening. "Poor Herbert. I am sorry if my silly little lamb hurt you." Then she takes Lolly back into the meadow.

After all that running – and jumping – and not catching butterflies – and swinging on Herbert's tail, Lolly is sleepy. She snoozes in the warm sunshine, and dreams of chasing fluffy clouds in the sky.

Happy Birthday Tessa

Today is Tessa the Tractor's birthday but she is still fast asleep in the barn. It is raining hard outside and the huge drops make a very loud pitter-patter on the tin roof. The noise wakes little Milly Mouse. "Come along, everyone," she squeaks. "We have to wrap up Tessa's birthday presents – quickly, before she wakes up!"

"But we haven't found her a present yet!" cries Monty.

"Oh dear, you are right," says Milly. They all think hard…
The rain slows and stops. Then the sun comes out. Tessa Tractor
is still snoring. "Let's run outside and see what we can find,"
suggests Monty. Off they scamper – and the first thing they
see is a HUGE puddle. "Tessa loves puddles!" cries Milly.

The little mice run back into the barn. Tessa is now wide awake.
They sing Happy Birthday to her and then they all shout,
"Come outside! We have a Big Surprise for you!"
Tessa is so excited to see the gigantic puddle. In she drives,
straight away, squealing with delight as the water splashes
everywhere and the mice run for cover.
"This is the BEST birthday present EVER," she laughs.
"Thank you SO MUCH!"

Duck Dreams

Duck is very little. He is the smallest duck in the farm pond.
Night falls. Duck dreams that he is a great big enormous duck;
he is as long as a dinosaur; he is as tall as a giant;
he is stronger than the tractor.
Then Freddy Frog snores a loud, croaky snore and
wakes up Duck. He is little tiny Duck once again.

The pond ripples and sways Duck gently to and fro. He drifts back
to sleep and dreams this time that he is tiny. He is shorter than
a daisy; he is smaller than a butterfly. The toads tower over him.
Then Freddy Frog snores another loud croaky snore
and Duck wakes up. "Perhaps I am not so very small after all.
I am certainly bigger than the daisies and the bees and
butterflies – and Freddy Frog!"

The sun is shining now.

"Hello!" quacks Mrs Duck. "Did you have nice dreams?"

"I don't know," answers Duck, "But I do know that I feel much bigger than when I went to sleep."

"You are perfect!" says his mum, "Just the right size for who you are now … and you will keep growing every day until you are taller than I am."

"Wow!" laughs happy little Duck.